WONDER BOOKS®

Respect

A Level Three Reader

By Kathryn Kyle

On the cover...
This boy is showing respect to a priest.

Published by The Child's World®, Inc.
PO Box 326
Chanhassen, MN 55317-0326
800-599-READ
www.childsworld.com

Special thanks to the Sanks, Rodriguez, and Campe families, and to the staff and students of Alessandro Volta and Shoesmith Elementary Schools for their help and cooperation in preparing this book.

Photo Credits
© 2003 Erik Dreyer/Stone: 26
© Jan Butchofsky-Houser/CORBIS: 25
© Myrleen Ferguson Cate/PhotoEdit: cover
© Romie Flanagan: 3, 5, 6, 9, 10, 13, 14, 17, 18, 21
© Underwood & Underwood/CORBIS: 22

Project Coordination: Editorial Directions, Inc.
Photo Research: Alice K. Flanagan

Library of Congress Cataloging-in-Publication Data
Kyle, Kathryn.
Respect / by Kathryn Kyle.
p. cm. — (Wonder books)
Includes index.
Summary: Suggests ways of showing respect for your school, friends, country, family, the environment, and others.
ISBN 1-56766-092-4 (library bound : alk. paper)
1. Respect—Juvenile literature. [1. Respect.]
I. Title. II. Wonder books (Chanhassen, Minn.)
BJ1533.R4 K95 2002
179'.9—dc21

2001007956

What is respect? Respect is showing that you value people or things. It is important to be respectful every day.

Showing respect can be about following rules. At school, you and some friends are working in the hall. It would be easy to be loud! But respect means working quietly. Respect is following the rules even when the teacher is not with you.

Showing respect can also mean taking care of **property**. In the library, a book is lying on the floor. You pick it up and put it on the cart. You are showing respect for the library's property.

You can show respect for other people at school, too. Your classmates are reading their reports. A friend is giving a boring report. You show respect for your friend by listening politely. You would want your friend to do the same for you.

Fish
Journal Writing
Today we learned how to write a sentence. We song our phonics song.
In math class, we found number patterns.
3. What could happen because of each choice?
A =?
B =?
4. Which is the best choice?

You can also show respect for your community. On the way home from school, you see some trash in the park. You pick it up and throw it away, even though it is not your trash. You are showing respect for the neighborhood.

You can show respect for your country, too. At the start of school, it is time to say the **Pledge of Allegiance**. You put your right hand over your heart. You are showing respect for the United States.

You can find many ways to show respect for your neighbors. Perhaps your neighbors have beautiful flowers. When you play soccer near their yard, you are careful not to run through the flowers. You are showing respect for your neighbors and their property.

At home, you can show respect for your parents by following their rules. They tell you to wear your **helmet** when you ride your bike to the park. You show respect for your parents by listening to them and wearing your helmet.

At home, you can show respect for your brothers and sisters. Your sister does not like you to go in her room when she is not home. When she is gone, you show respect by staying out of her room.

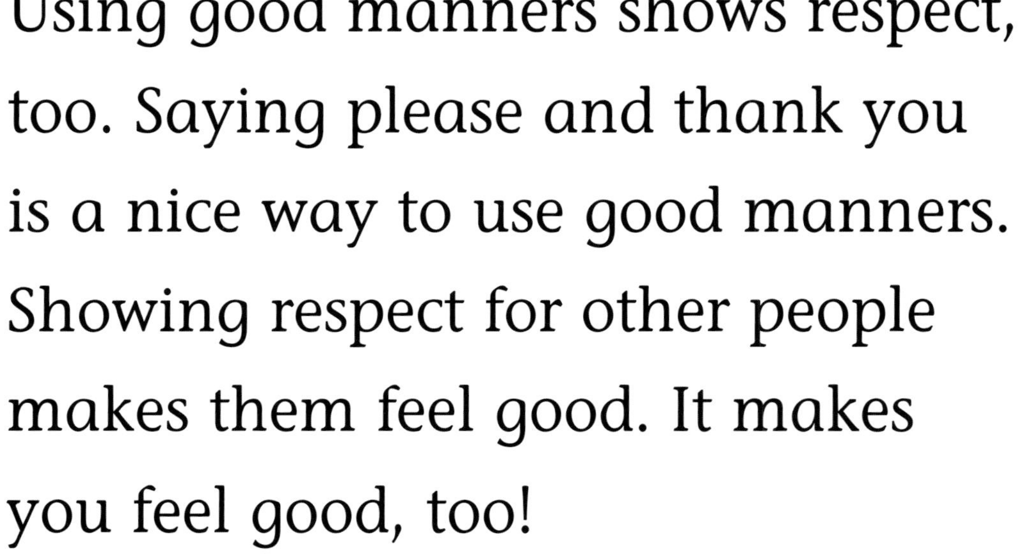

Using good manners shows respect, too. Saying please and thank you is a nice way to use good manners. Showing respect for other people makes them feel good. It makes you feel good, too!

rld of Reading
y, December 1, 2001

Many people in history have shown respect for others. One of these people was Gutzon Borglum. He was an artist. He was asked to **carve** a large **monument** in the hills of South Dakota. Borglum wanted to honor four of the country's presidents. He wanted to carve the faces of George Washington, Thomas Jefferson, Theodore Roosevelt, and Abraham Lincoln.

← This is a picture of Gutzon Borglum.

Borglum worked on the monument from 1927 until he died in 1941. The monument is called Mount Rushmore. Borglum spent his life working to show respect for four of the presidents. However, many people believe Borglum shouldn't have built Mount Rushmore where he did. The monument was built on **sacred** Indian land taken by the government.

This is a picture of Mount Rushmore today. →

It is important to show respect. Showing respect for each other helps people get along. It helps us to work together and to be friends. How have you shown respect today?

At Home

- Put your brother's or sister's toys away after you are done playing with them.
- If the door to someone's room is closed, knock before going in.
- Always ask if it is okay before using something that belongs to your parents.

At School

- Hold the door open for someone who is entering a building with you.
- Keep your schoolbooks neat and clean.
- Apologize if you bump into someone in the hallway.

In Your Community

- Say hello to your neighbors when you see them outside.
- Follow the rules when you are playing on a team at the park.
- Sit quietly when you are at the movies.

Glossary

carve (KARV)
To carve is to make a shape out of a piece of stone or other material.

helmet (HEL-met)
A helmet is a hard hat that protects your head when you are playing.

monument (MON-yuh-ment)
A monument is a building or statue that honors a person, a group, or an event.

Pledge of Allegiance
(PLEJ uv uh-LEE-jents)
The Pledge of Allegiance is a promise to support the United States. It is often recited in school classrooms.

property (PROP-er-tee)
Property is something that is owned by someone.

sacred (SAY-kred)
When something is sacred, it is very important. Many sacred things have to do with religion.

Index

To Find Out More

Books

Klingel, Cynthia, and Robert B. Noyed. *Mount Rushmore.* Chanhassen, Minn.: The Child's World, 2001.

Milford, Susan. *Hands around the World: 365 Creative Ways to Encourage Cultural Awareness and Global Respect.* Charlotte, Vt.: Williamson Publishing, 1992.

Owens, Tomas S. *Mount Rushmore.* New York: Rosen Publishing Group, 1997.

Parr, Todd. *It's Okay to Be Different.* Boston: Little Brown Children's Books, 2001.

Web Sites

Defining Diversity, Prejudice, and Respect
http://kidshealth.org/kid/feeling/emotion/diversity.html
To learn about treating people respectfully.

Hero Quest
http://www.uen.org/utahlink/activities/view_activity.cgi?activity_id=7077
To explore what qualities make a hero.

Note to Parents and Educators

Welcome to Wonder Books®! These books provide text at three different levels for beginning readers to practice and strengthen their reading skills. Additionally, the use of nonfiction text provides readers the valuable opportunity to *read to learn*, not just to learn to read.

These leveled readers allow children to choose books at their level of reading confidence and performance. Nonfiction Level One books offer beginning readers simple language, word choice, and sentence structure as well as a word list. Nonfiction Level Two books feature slightly more difficult vocabulary, longer sentences, and longer total text. In the back of each Nonfiction Level Two book are an index and a list of books and Web sites for finding out more information. Nonfiction Level Three books continue to extend word choice and length of text. In the back of each Nonfiction Level Three book are a glossary, an index, and a list of books and Web sites for further research.

State and national standards in reading and language arts emphasize using nonfiction at all levels of reading development. Wonder Books® fill the historical void in nonfiction material for primary grade readers with the additional benefit of a leveled text.

About the Author

Kathryn Kyle has taught elementary school and writes extensively for children. She lives in Minnesota.